This edition published by Parragon Books Ltd in 2017

Parragon Books Ltd
Chartist House
15–17 Trim Street
Bath BA1 1HA, UK
www.parragon.com

ISBN 978-1-4748-7643-8

Printed in China

Bath · New York · Cologne · Melbourne · Delhi
Hong Kong · Shenzhen · Singapore

It was race day in Tennessee! Lightning McQueen, hotshot racer and winner of seven Piston Cups, was in action. He was leading the field in front of a packed stadium once again. But as Lightning prepared to take the chequered flag, a mysterious racer pipped him to the post!

Jackson Storm introduced himself after the race. "It was a pleasure to *beat* you!" Storm teased.

Storm was a sleek racer who belonged to the next generation of high-tech cars. Race after race, Storm finished in first place. Lightning just couldn't keep up.

Soon came the last race of the season. Lightning was determined that this race would be his.

After a speedy pit stop, Lightning pulled into the lead – only for Storm to blaze past him seconds later.

"Enjoy your retirement," Storm shouted out.

"No!" yelled Lightning, revving his engine loudly. But he pushed himself too hard. Lightning went into overdrive and lost control.

Months passed as Lightning sat alone in Doc's garage in Radiator Springs. "It's safe to say that Lightning McQueen's racing days are over," the radio crackled.

Lightning switched off the radio and watched a video of a race – the one where Doc Hudson, his old crew chief and mentor, had crashed.

Lightning hadn't raced since his own big crash. But he decided that he wasn't ready to quit just yet. He had to speak to his Rust-eze sponsors, Dusty and Rusty.

The next day, Lightning travelled to the brand-new Rust-eze Racing Centre to discover that Dusty and Rusty had sold Rust-eze and the number 95 to a business car named Sterling.

Sterling showed Lightning around the racing centre. Lightning was amazed – he'd never seen anything like it before.

Lightning looked up at a yellow
car racing super-fast on a special
machine called a simulator.
It allowed racers to train on
a virtual racetrack.
"Who's the racer?" Lightning
asked Sterling.
"No, no, no, she's a
trainer," said Sterling.
"Cruz Ramirez – best
trainer in the business."

Cruz was going to be Lightning's new trainer. She was a cool and calm car, and if anyone could help Lightning win races again, it was Cruz Ramirez!

Lightning was bursting to get going on the simulator, but Cruz had other ideas.

"We need to save your energy," Cruz explained. "We'll work on your speed after your nap."

But when Lightning saw his chance, he sped away from Cruz and drove up the simulator ramp.

Sterling arrived to watch his star racer in action. But Lightning lost control, and crashed through the simulator screen!

Sterling wanted to pull Lightning from the race, but Lightning begged for another chance. Sterling agreed, on one condition: if Lightning didn't win the Florida 500, it was to be his last race.

Cruz followed Lightning out onto Fireball Beach to track his speed. Lightning was done with treadmills and simulators – he needed to get his tyres dirty.

Lightning raced to the pier at top speed. Cruz had planned to drive alongside him to track his time, but she couldn't keep up with him – her wheels just spun in the soft sand!

Lightning tried to show Cruz what to do, but she kept getting stuck. Then at last, she tracked him all the way to the pier. But Lightning's top speed was still slower than Storm's.

Lightning wished Doc was there to help him. Then
Lightning had an idea. Doc might not be around anymore,
but the car who coached him was. That was it! Lightning
had to find Doc's old crew chief – Smokey.

Mack took Lightning and Cruz to Thomasville – Doc
Hudson's old racetrack. When they arrived,
Smokey introduced Lightning and Cruz to his friends:
three racing legends who had competed with Doc.

Smokey told a story about a famous race,
where Doc had flipped over another racer to
take the victory! Cruz and Lightning were amazed.
    Smokey had some wise words for Lightning.
    "You'll never be as fast as Storm," said Smokey.
"But you can be smarter than him."

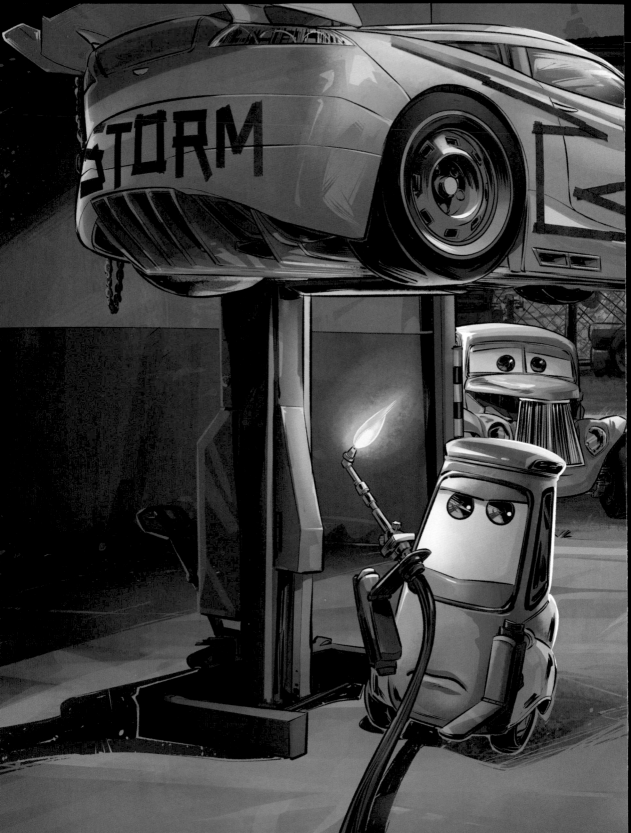

To beat Storm, Lightning was going to need a racing partner. So Guido and the Legends fitted a spoiler and racing tyres to Cruz and transformed her into 'Jackson Storm 2.0'! She was ready to go, but this time as a racer, not a trainer.

Smokey gave Cruz a head start. They took off together, but Lightning couldn't catch Cruz. There was work to do if Lightning was going to beat the real Storm.

Smokey trained Lightning and Cruz hard.
They pulled heavy trailers, dodged bales of
hay and even steered through a stampede of
tractors. Lightning was feeling better than ever.

In their last practice before the big race, Lightning went out fast, but Cruz caught up and left him for dust.

Lightning was stunned. Even after all his hard work, he still wasn't fast enough. But it was too late for another race – it was time to head to Florida.

The day of the Florida 500 race arrived. Cruz and all Lightning's friends had come to watch.

Lightning rolled to the back of the grid. To everyone's surprise, Lightning made a speedy start.

"Show 'em how the old guys race!" shouted Smokey, who was acting as Lightning's crew chief. Lightning pushed hard and began overtaking the racers in front.

In the pits, Sterling ordered Cruz to take off her racing tyres and head back to the training centre. "You're a trainer, Cruz. Not a racer," he said.

Lightning heard Sterling's harsh words over his headset. As he raced, all he could think about was Cruz: her speed on the simulator, all their races in training and how Cruz had beaten him every time.

Suddenly, two cars crashed up ahead. Lightning swerved and headed immediately into the pits.

"I need Cruz back here!" he told Smokey. Cruz was a racer, no matter what anyone said.

In the pits, Lightning told his team to work on Cruz instead of him.

Guido, Luigi and Ramone worked fast, and soon Cruz was ready. Her spoiler shone and the number 95 glistened on her side. She looked like a racer from bumper to bumper.

"Today's the day, Cruz. You're getting your shot," Lightning told her. "I started this race and you're going to finish it."

The crowd gasped when they saw Cruz join the race wearing Lightning's number. The green flag dropped and they were off!

Cruz started slowly, but Lightning knew what to do. He asked Smokey to tell Cruz to remember their Thomasville training and imagine the other racers were tractors.

It worked! Cruz began overtaking the cars one by one.

With one lap to go, Cruz drew up alongside Storm.
She tried to pass him, but Storm spotted the move
and rammed her against a wall.

"You don't belong on this track!" he yelled.

"YES ... I ... DO!" she cried.

Remembering Doc's move, Cruz flipped up and over
Storm. She touched down again on the track in front
of Storm, and then crossed the finish line in first place.

The crowd went wild, and Lightning couldn't have been
more proud. Then, Lightning and Cruz were announced
as joint-winners. Lightning hadn't lost the race so he didn't
have to retire!

He knew his racing days weren't over, but for now,
Lightning was devoted to getting Cruz ready for her next
big race. It didn't matter who was the racer and who was
the trainer, Lightning and Cruz were both true champions.